14 Days

W9-BAJ-213

# WINTER'S TALES

WRITTEN BY MICHAEL FOREMAN
ILLUSTRATED BY FREIRE WRIGHT

Published by Doubleday & Company Inc., Garden City, New York

**Library of Congress Cataloging in Publication Data**
Foreman, Michael, 1938– Winter's Tales. **Summary:** A collection of six brief illustrated stories celebrating the spirit of Christmas.
1. Christmas Stories. (1. Christmas Stories 2. Short Stories) 1. Wright, Freire. 11. Title.
PZ7. F7583 W1 (E) 79-1862.
ISBN 0-385-15460-7 (TRADE) 0-385-15461-5 (PREBOUND)    Library of Congress Catalog Card Number  79-1862

FOR EILEEN

# CHRISTMAS COMES BUT ONCE A YEAR

"It's not much fun being a scarecrow," thought the scarecrow. "I'm out in all kinds of weather. My clothes are a mess. It's lonely too."

"The farmer occasionally gives me some new stuffing and a little gossip,
   but that's all."

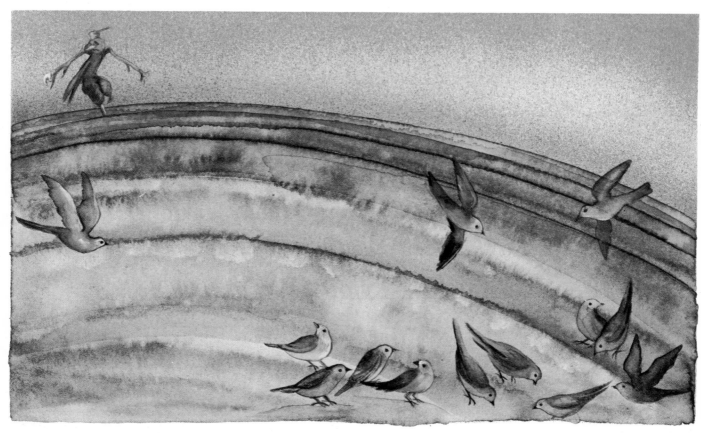

"Even the birds stay away from me!
   It must be great to be a bird. Free to move around, to go beyond the hills.
   Free to fly, to see the world. Not stuck in one place like me."

So the scarecrow stood still while everything around him changed.
Season followed season, until on Christmas Eve, it began to snow.

It snowed and snowed. "Just my luck," groaned the scarecrow. "What a cold
Christmas I'm going to have."

But on Christmas morning, everything around him looked different.
There was a white blanket over fields, trees and hills. The scarecrow, too,
had changed. The birds no longer stayed away from him. They flocked around.
They perched all over him and sang all day.
The scarecrow was overjoyed. "It's wonderful," he decided.
"Christmas changes everyone, even me! If only Christmas came every week,
like Wednesday. Or every day, like the dawn."

# FAIR PLAY

"Goodbye, dear," said Santa Claus. "I'm off now."

"It's all right for you," said his wife. "I work all year wrapping presents and cooking your dinners and you never take me anywhere."

"I'll take you to the movies after Christmas, or maybe to a hockey game," said Santa Claus.

"My life is a hockey game and the movies have been closed down," replied Mrs. Claus. "It's not fair. Let me help you deliver the presents. It's time I saw something of the world."

"Yes, dear, of course, dear," said Santa Claus.

Mrs. Claus put on all her overcoats and all her husband's socks and then they flew up into the night.

"I'm going this way around the world," said Santa Claus, "to keep up
   with the night."
"I know that," said Mrs. Claus, "I'm not dumb. But you should have
   turned left at Norway. It's a short cut. And what a mess you've got the
   presents in. They're all mixed up! That policeman in Huddersfield isn't going
   to be too happy with the navy blue dress you left him."
"I don't know," laughed Santa Claus, "it matches his cap."
"You're even worse at delivering presents than at changing fuses,"
   said Mrs. Claus as they landed back home.
"All right!" shouted Santa Claus, "if you're so smart, next year you do it!"
"All right," she said, "I will."

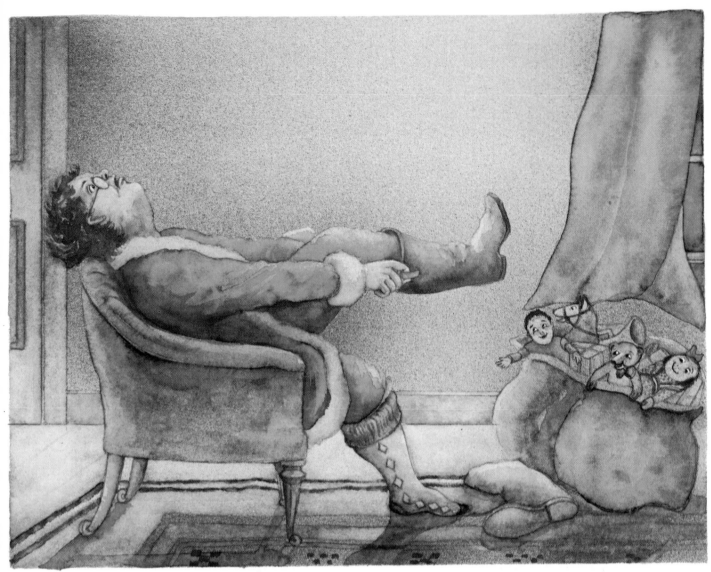

And she did.
Next year, she dressed up in Santa's famous outfit so she would look like Santa
if any naughty children weren't asleep.

And she delivered the presents herself.

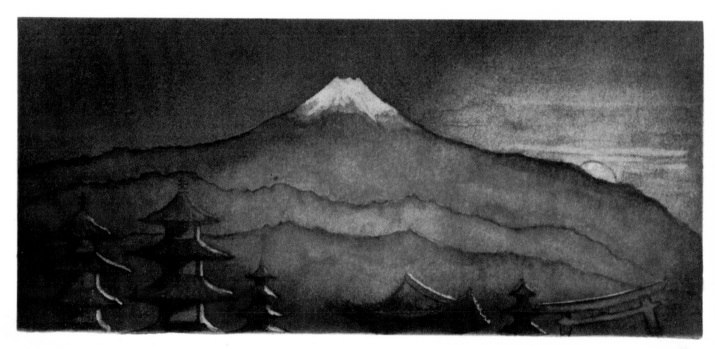

And when she got home, Santa Claus was still in bed.
"Well," he said slyly, "where's my present?"
"You will get your present after you have cooked the Christmas turkey!"
replied Mrs. Claus.
"Turnabout is fair play," yelled the turkey, jumping out of the window. "Isn't it time
*I* saw something of the world?"

# WANT! WANT! WANT!

Once there was a tiny beetle who lived with lots of other beetles high in the rafters.
In winter, when all the other beetles were peacefully sleeping until spring,
this tiny beetle lay awake, making lists of all the things he wanted.
'Want, Want, Want!' his friends called him. At last, he tossed and turned so much
that he fell out of bed. He fell and fell, but being tiny, he landed lightly.

It was the first time he'd been away from home in winter and he was afraid.
He could see a chain of cold, white mountains, surrounding him. Now he knew wh
he really wanted. He wanted to go home and wait for spring. He wanted his friends
He wanted something to eat. Want, Want, Want.

Near the mountains was a man. "Excuse me, but I'm lost," said the beetle.
But the man seemed rooted to the ground and did not answer.
"Frozen stiff," decided the beetle, "I must keep on going."

He followed the mountains, hoping to find a pass through them. Hour after hour
he dragged himself across the white wilderness. Then he saw a big bird on a log.
"Maybe he will be my friend. Maybe he has food. He may even help me get home!"
thought the tiny beetle, hopefully.
But the bird took no notice of him. (Birds can be very snobbish sometimes.)

Exhausted, the tiny beetle finally gave up hope of finding his way and began to nibble a shelter for himself in the log. Chocolate! The beetle couldn't believe it and nibbled again. The log was made of chocolate! He did a couple of cartwheels and kissed the ground. The ground was delicious! He scampered around and had a mouthful of mountain.

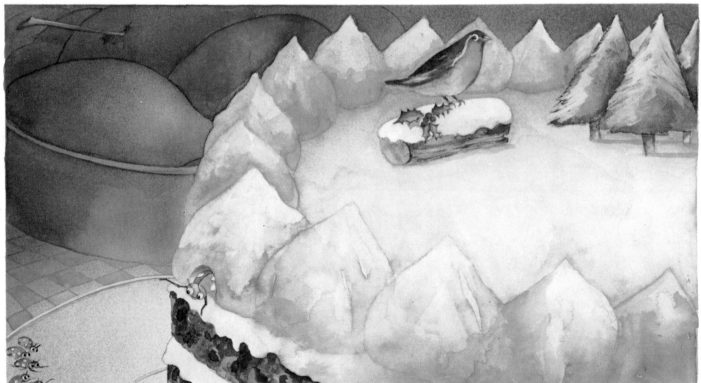

Suddenly he heard his name. It was a search party of his beetle friends, calling 'Want Want Want!'
They led the tiny beetle back to the safety of their home and they all slept until spring. When he awoke, it was to a world of sunshine and flowers, where at last, he wanted for nothing.

# THE OGRE'S HEART

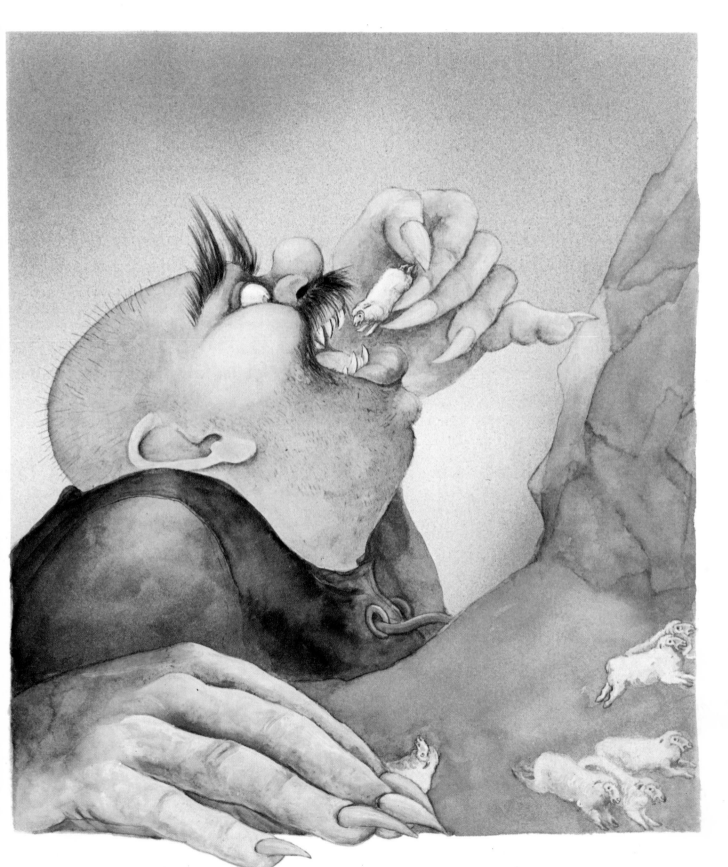

The people of the mountain were terrified of the ogre. When he was hungry he
stole their sheep and stripped the fruit from their orchards.
At Christmas time he was worse and even stole their turkeys and mince pies.

One Christmas Eve, the ogre was sleeping in the valley and dreaming of all the good things he would steal next day.

Santa Claus had delivered all the presents and he was feeling very weary,
when he found what he thought was one more chimney.
He searched his sack but could find only a few pieces of ribbon, mistletoe and holly.

"Better than nothing," he decided and clambered down into the dark.
"This is a very strange house," he thought as he followed a long passage into a
  huge, vaulted hall.

On one side was a big machine which boomed and rumbled.
"It must be some kind of organ," Santa decided.

He draped holly and mistletoe and ribbons all over the machine while he whistled
*Jingle Bells* to keep himself awake.
Then he climbed back to his reindeer and flew home, still whistling.

Next morning, the villagers were amazed to see the ogre dancing through the valley singing *Jingle Bells*. "Merry Christmas," he yelled. "Merry Christmas everyone!" "Maybe," said one old man wisely, "the spirit of Christmas has touched his heart at last." The other villagers agreed and after waving cheerfully to the ogre, they went home to their Christmas turkeys and hot mince pies.

# The Decorated Forest

Every year, the morning before Christmas, the woodcutters came to cut down the tallest, straightest tree in the forest. The tree was taken to the village square and an old man would come bringing stars and ribbons and all kinds of decorations from his workshop in the mountains.

This year, as usual, the woodcutters had cut down the tallest, straightest tree and set it up in the square. The children waited for the decorations. But the old man did not come.

He had set off from the snowy peaks, but near the center of the forest he had sat down for a rest. There, he listened to the birds arguing and complaining to a large owl.

The owl, in a very bent and twisted tree, was shrugging his shoulders and shaking his head, saying, "I told you soo, I told you soo . . ."
"But we have nowhere to live," cried the birds. "They've chopped down our tree."
"Of course," said the owl. "I told you not to live in the tallest, straightest tree, but you wouldn't listen. You thought it would be higher than everyone else and you always laughed at my home. However, you are welcome to stay with me over Christmas."

The old man was moved by the kindness and wisdom of the old owl and wanted to help make Christmas in the old tree a success. He chose a few of the most beautiful stars from his sack and began to decorate the branches. The owl was delighted and the other birds sang as each new star was added. Meanwhile, the children in the village were still waiting. They waited all morning and most of the afternoon.

At last, they set out to look for the old man. But they did not come back. Later, a search party was sent to look for the children, and finally the whole village went in search of the search party.

j37214

They found the search party and the children and the old man and all the animals
and birds dancing in the light of the moon. And in the middle stood the most
beautiful tree they had ever seen. The villagers hesitated for a second and then

they too joined in. The owl officially welcomed the Mayor and villagers
to the forest and everyone danced. Then food was brought and at midnight there
was carol singing which went on all the way home.

That Christmas Day, and every Christmas afterward, was celebrated in the forest.
The villagers and animals hid gifts for each other. The old man made more
decorations than ever, and every tree had a star.
But best of all, there was no need to chop down any more of the tallest,
straightest trees in the forest.

# A CHRISTMAS KNIGHT

Among the mice in the big house there was a famous hunter. He knew Christmas was the best time to hunt for tasty morsels. Each year he would creep around the kitchen, seeing what the cook was preparing, so that he could provide plenty of food for his parents, aunts and uncles.

But this year was different. He had just married and wanted to give his wife a Christmas present of real beauty as a token of his love.

He knew that people got such wonderful gifts from colored paper packages, so early on Christmas morning he inspected the dining table.
There was a paper package beside each empty plate.

The hunter began dragging one of the prettiest packages toward his home. Suddenly, the cat of the house appeared and pounced!
"Help me!" cried the hunter to his family. All the mice took hold of the colored package and pulled desperately.

"CRACK!"
The tug of war ended with a tremendous explosion.

The cat was shocked. And he fled as a most ferocious and fearless mouse in shining armor dashed out to attack. The hunter and his family cheered as the

knight chased the cat around the dining room . . .

through the kitchen and out into the snow. Neither was ever seen again.

Later that Christmas Day, the hunter found a gift suitable for his wife.
It shone with all the beauty of her eyes and the mystery of her smile.
"Husband dear," she said, "I don't know what it is, but it's what I've always wanted."
And throughout the years its brightness unlocked the warm memories
of their first Christmas together.